IMAGINE THAT

Licensed exclusively to Imagine That Publishing Ltd
Tide Mill Way, Woodbridge, Suffolk, IP12 1AP, UK
www.imaginethat.com
Text and illustrations copyright © 2018 Rebecca Elliott.
All rights reserved
0 2 4 6 8 9 7 5 3 1
Manufactured in Zhejiang, China

Written and illustrated by Rebecca Elliott

Cub's First Winter

by Rebecca Elliot

It was the first day of winter
and Cub could not sleep. "OK," said Mom.
"One more forest walk before bed. Come on..."

"Why are all the trees bare?" asked Cub.

"So we can have
fun in the leaves!"
answered Mom.

And the snow clouds
gathered in the sky.

"Why are my friends asleep all the time?" asked Cub. "Ssshhh! So we can laugh at their snoring!" giggled Mom.

And the first snowflake fell to the ground.

"Why are the birds going on vacation?" asked Cub.
"So they can tell us all about their journey when they come back!" said Mom.

And the snow began to gently fall.

"Why is it so windy?" asked Cub.
"So we can be blown around together
in the tall grass!" laughed Mom.

And the snow drifted down.

"Why can I see my own breath?" asked Cub.
"So we can puff like steam trains!" puffed Mom.

And the snow began to settle on the ground.

"Why is the river solid?" asked Cub.
"So we can slide and dance on it!" exclaimed Mom.

And the snow fell more quickly.

"Why does the sun disappear so early?" asked Cub.
"So we can look up at the stars for longer," explained Mom.

And the snow got deeper and deeper.

"Why is everything white?" asked Cub.

"Oh no!" gasped Mom.
"Quick, follow me before we lose our way home!"

And back they went through the white forest, over the white river, up and down the white rocks, and around and around the white trees until, at last, they found their way home!

"Why is it so c-c-cold?"
asked Cub.

"So we can
snuggle up tight,"
whispered Mom,
with a smile.

"Why am I so tired?"
yawned Cub.
"Because it is sleepy time,"
murmured Mom.
"Goodnight little cub."